MW01047416

LastNight
Chapter 1

MrDaniel Evans

MrDaniel Evans

Copyright © 2014 Daniel Evans

All rights reserved.

ISBN:
ISBN-13: 9781072694854

DEDICATION

This project is dedicated to my mother who never quits. She showed me that dreams do not have an age limit and she always told me to keep cooking no matter how backed up in life you get. Thank you, mom, for being there for me and for loving me. I love you.

MrDaniel Evans

CONTENTS

ACKNOWLEDGMENTS

Thank you to every person who has provided some type of inspiration for this project. Every character is based on someone real in my life, you know who you are. I thank you for allowing us to spend those moments together and being a muse for my creativity. Thank You.

LASTNIGHT

I can remember that night like it was last night. I can recall everything about that night. The way the atmosphere had a romantic glow, the way the air crawled on my skin, the way the rain accentuated the end of a wonderful but dreadful night; a night that I will never forget. A night which allotted regret an outlet to be repeated without any regret if given another opportunity. I loved and hated that night. I wish that night would have never happened but I'm glad that it did.

My day was going like any other day. Normality was my humble complex.

I was satisfied.

My life had a routine with love as a threshold.

My love was solid.

My love was guaranteed.

As I was driving home I knew how the day was going to end, for my routine was en route and I was content with that. Although I felt my romantic spirit evaporating out of my pores, the perspiration that

accumulated from events to come would have been
nothing not previously experienced; it would have
been routine for nights that I felt like this.

I was prepared for that.

I look forward to those moments to come. My life
was filled with satisfaction and I was satisfied with
that,

until She called.

Now she is special in every way a person can be
considered to be special to me. She is my friend that's
been in my life for a while. She is a very dear friend
that I value highly and hopefully, she will always be in
my life.

My mood changes when I answer the phone for her.
Her "Hey" is vibrant and energetic as it echoes through
my surround sound. High energy pours out of my
speakers as we converse for we haven't talked in a
minute. Typical how you been's and what you been up
too's. Nothing out of the ordinary for two close friends
that have let time accumulate between interactions.
Every time I talk to She I realize how much I miss
talking to her.

I have a love for Her that will never go away.

As we geared toward the end of our conversation, there's a slight pause. Neither one of us wants to hang up but we know that it is necessary to continue what we have.

As I decide to take control of the hanging up situation, she interrupts my faint 'I'll talk to you later' with a 'come over tonight.'

Her come over tonight was more of an unsure statement. Her tone is mellow which creates a type of sex appeal and her diction is low from unsureness and hopefulness. Come over tonight was a statement that's been silently lingering over our heads for years but neither one of us wanted to address that cloud because of the hidden terms and conditions that allow our relationship to flow the way it does. Up until now, I was safe from how I felt.

There's a pause as I drive and think. I think about having some unexpected excitement with her. Then I drive and think some more. I think about keeping my routine of satisfactory that I've become accustomed to.

At the conclusion of my thoughts, she interrupts the
silence by saying it's okay if I can't come with such
sincere disappointment that dwells in my ears and
outweighs my heart to the point of submission. Right
then and there I made up my mind that I was going to
see my friend; my friend that I care for;
my friend that I will always love.
The conversation is concluded with an, "okay see you
when you get here," that chills my body and freezes
my mind with only thoughts of her. I can feel the
unforeseen anticipation begin to increase my heart rate.
For some reason I am nervous.
I have to concentrate harder on the road for I am
seeing replays of previous conversations ending
between us which have never left an emotion such as
nervousness igniting, ready to explode into giddiness.
But why was I giddy, why were my arms filled with
goosebumps. I guess deep down the answer is hidden
in the subconscious communication between my
untapped feelings that I have for She and She's hidden
meaning behind the statement 'come over.'

As I'm driving along a few calls ignite my phone but none are answered for I am concentrating on She. She is on my mind. She is my current route. Certain calls were ignored with slight hesitation, but I didn't want anything to deter me from my altered destination. All I could think about was She. The only thing I wanted to think about was She.

Evening strikes as I pull up to her place. I glare at the house through the windshield of a parked car. There is no hesitance circulating through my brain cells, I'm just enjoying the moment of being outside of her house. I am enjoying the fact that I'm here about to see my friend; my beautiful friend; my friend that brings joy into my life every time I encounter her; my friend that I love to be around.

A few marinating moments pass and I'm still in the car. Apart of me is prepared to see her, another side is pleading for me to leave; screaming for me to back out of her driveway and head back to normality. Confused about what I want to do I decide to make a decision.

I put my car in reverse.

My thoughts must have escaped the interior of my
vehicle because the mouth of her house suddenly
begins to open, and after it's movements, it is a
beautiful woman waving, signaling for me to come in.
Without hesitation, I put my car back in park and
comply. As I walk towards the beautiful smiling face
that is greeting me at the entrance of her home, the
beauty that is drawing me in, is starting to seem so
wrong. The hug that I'm embraced with is feeling too
good. The body that my arms are wrapped around is
feeling too soft. The voice that is spelling out my
name, is sounding too wonderful. This moment is
feeling so right it has to be wrong, but to have this
beautiful woman embrace me with all this energy and
excitement is a wonderful feeling that I haven't felt in a
while. I except her warm embrace and pull her into me.
For the moment I live in her arms. But this moment
can't last that long for I have a routine that was en
route and I have to get back to normality.
So I am here for a few minutes but then I must leave.
The garage door slams while we share a 'haven't seen
each other in a while' embrace. She leads me through

the downstairs of her home explaining that she didn't think I was coming due to previous stand-ups by both of us which is why daily household chores where being completed and regular house wear covered her curves. Everything is going safe and smooth as she guides me through the house on an unofficial tour. I'm feeling confident about my brief visit until I turn the corner on the second set of steps.

On the second set of steps, the mood changes and the atmosphere becomes heavy. On the second set of steps, there are lit candles and dim lights. On the second set of steps, She's walk becomes sexier, her grip becomes tighter on my wrist, her eyes lock into my eyes as if she's trying to mentally prepare me for what's about to happen.

At the top of the steps, I got hit with the realization that her come over tonight wasn't for talking.

Apparently, we've talked too much.

Candles lined in a row continue to guide our future past the living room, where relaxing music is escaping into my spirit, and into a complete candlelit dining

room where a five-course meal awaits me at the head
of the table.

Her lips spoke my mind when her words 'you're
going to enjoy this' jumps from her tongue and dives
into my body. What she speaks bounces hard from ear
to ear till I realized that she wasn't talking about just
the food. At that moment I felt that I knew she knew
what she was doing. Every word, every comment, even
the way we briefly locked eyes before she walked
away. The way she walked away, the food in front of
me, everything was having me trapped into her web
and I loved it. I loved every minute of it. I loved the
fact that someone would take time out of their life and
think about me. I loved the fact that this was out of my
normal routine. I was overly satisfied. I was excited
because it was She that was doing this. I didn't know
she had this in her. Right now She has my full
attention as she walks back into the room with a
rectangular shaped bucket of steaming hot water and
places it down by my feet. She then removes my shoes
and socks, puts them to the side, rolls up my pants, and

places my feet in the water so I can relax and enjoy my
dinner.

At this point, I have to keep myself calm and attempt
to take this treatment in-stride. I allow myself to
breathe once she leaves the room to let me finish
eating. I've never been treated in such a manner. As if
I'm a king. Like the hours I put in at work are worth it.
Now, this would make a man run home after work. I'm
not expecting to be treated like this every day but
breaking a normal cycle every now-and-then would
bring excitement to the dull word home. But either
way there's a stream of normality that my life is
currently indulged in and I need to continue my flow
home. The food was good but now I have to leave.

I remember glancing around the dining room in search
of my shoes but couldn't find them. So I exited the
same way I entered but the candles didn't guide me out
the door the same way they guided me to dinner. They
were now making their way upstairs with roses in
between and there was a letter on the post that said
read before you leave.

With how relaxed my body felt and with how good
the texture of the roses felt underneath my feet;
I felt obliged to do so.

I've been nothing but impressed with Her so far and
even the letter didn't disappoint. Everything that she
touches at this moment seems to glow. The letter has
an enduring scent that draws me in and makes me put
it to my face so I inhale until I could no longer breathe.
Even her handwriting was elegant as she pointed out
that my shoes were by the door or the rest of the
evening can continue upstairs; it was my choice.
What was I to do? I looked upstairs, but my mind said
to go put on my shoes. With one glance at my shoes, I
was fatally shot by disappointment. How was I going
to leave in the middle of a memorable experience? I
knew what was on the other side of the door; my
normal life with normal life issues and problems.
Upstairs was a memory of a lifetime, regardless of how
it played out. Everything that has happened up until
this point was forever going to be on my mind and I
thank her for that. Now I could say this is the end and
leave or I could stay and create a beautiful alternate

ending. So I stood there and began to think. Then I stood to think some more. As I formulated a conclusion in my mind, it began to rain. I could feel the heavy but soft rain change the atmosphere. I heard the rain hit the house with a slight melody that gave a rhythm to how I felt. I relaxed and closed my eyes for a minute and took an appreciation for the music of the rain. I felt like the rain was singing to me. I felt as if the rain answered my question on what to do. So I let the rhythm guide my feet to where I should go. I let the rhythm guide me upstairs to be with my friend.

My walk upstairs was long and short. With every step taken, I became extremely relaxed and overly excited. My feelings about my friend were intertwining. I couldn't believe I was headed to her bedroom. The only other time I've seen where she lays her head was when I was being a good friend and helped her move in. But what's going to happen when I entered her bedroom again? Have we reached this point in our friendship? There's an attraction between the opposite sexes that naturally exists, but can our type of relationship survive a night of bliss, what did she expect from this? Can one night change what we have? For every action, there's a reaction and as I placed my hand on the door and slowly pushed it open, I was wondering whether the action I was committing` was going to be uplifting or deflating. Either way, I was ready, willing, and tired of waiting. I was eager to find out what the relationship between She and I was really about.

As the door slides open, I am hit again with another aroma that has my mind just as relaxed as my feet.

Candles are the only source of light and rain and familiar slow love songs are the only sounds available. Standing as the eye of this tornado of love was She.

And she was beautiful.

Her attire accompanied my business attire which threw me off for a pleasant surprise. A button down, slacks, and heels weren't on my mind but at the same time it eased the pressure; it allowed me to keep myself together.

As I entered her bedroom, she grabs my arm and directs me to where she wants me to be; on the bed. The pillows are propped so I can sit up as I sit back. I

17

put my feet up as I lay back, then she hands me a glass of wine and whispers one word to me; relax. The wind from her whisper enters my ear as if it was alive and looking for every switch that it could hit to turn me on. The combination of her voice, her wind, and with the slight touch of her soft lips barely grazing my ear as she spoke, she found what it took and broke the levy which caused my blood to start rushing so all of me could give her the full attention that she required.

For whatever she wanted I was hers.

As the next song began, she steps back so I can view the entire her and she begins to move as if the beat from the music caught her body in a current that forced her to sway seductively from side to side.

With every sip of the wine, I became more and more mesmerized. I couldn't take my eyes off her.

I didn't want to take my eyes off her.

Her arms, waist, and her hips were all moving in a different direction at the same time. Her hair that was pinned up was now draping over her shoulders. Her shirt that was buttoned up was now open. She was teasing me and I loved it. And I wanted more. And she gave me more. She gave me exactly what I wanted. She played on the fact that my eyes drove along her curves. When she went down and came up, dropped her shirt and loosened her pants, my eyes stalked her movements. My eyes told her exactly what she wanted to know; that I wanted her, that I needed her, that I needed this moment with her. My eyes told her at this moment nobody else was on my mind except her.

That nobody else mattered except her.

With every song, she revealed more of herself until she was down to her lingerie and heels. With every movement in her lingerie, she gave me clues for her satisfaction to be fulfilled. Her hands were guiding our future, instructing me how to explore her body. When she touched herself in certain areas her facials expressions emphasized the importance of that spot. When certain areas were felt by her hands, her body language screamed to me not to forget that spot when it's my turn to be her hands; when it's my turn for my feelings to erupt and for us to physically express to one another what we have for each other. What we've always had for each other.

And when it became my turn I didn't forget anything her body told me. When it became my turn I overly exerted every spot that required my attention. I played close attention to her body and intertwined our movements to become one. When it became my turn I expressed to her the hidden feelings that I've always had in the crevices of my heart. When it became my turn those feelings manifested themselves through my hands, tongue, and body.

Every touch, every kiss, every movement yelled loudly that I've always wanted her, that I hated the space that comes between us; that I think about her constantly and missed her badly whenever our separate lives came into play; that the feelings I had inside where real although they were surrounded by the boundaries of friendship.

Every inch of her body knew that I had a deep love inside of me that desired to be seen, that desired to be recognized, and she verbally and physically recognized them. The expressions from her body revealed to me that my point was being made, that my love was not going in vain, and that she felt everything I was telling

her, that she accepted and welcomed my feelings into
her body. She accepted and welcomed me into her
body and I entered. I entered her and became one with
her. I became one with her. I became one with my
friend.

The moment I entered her, I replayed every step it
took for us to be at this moment and I thanked her.

With my body, I thanked her for treating me like a
king, for giving me what I needed, for showing me that
I am worth her thoughts. That I am worth a phone call
when she desires love, when she doesn't want to be
alone, when attention from a man becomes her needs; I
thanked her for thinking about me.

From her lungs escaped harmonies of gratitude.
From her lungs escaped the overflow of satisfaction
that was being produced by the symphony of romance
composed from the rhythm of our love.

Our music was beautiful.

She was beautiful. We were beautiful together. We
made love in the purest form. We made love the way it
was supposed to be made. We were in sync from

MrDaniel Evans

beginning to end. We created a moment that neither
one of us would ever forget.

I created a beautiful moment in time with my friend.

Lying next to my friend with her head on my chest
and watching replays of us in my mind was almost just
as beautiful as creating our moment in time.

Her hand rubs my shoulder and chest as I stroke her
hair and rub her head as we talk. Her voice is just as
soft to my ears as her skin is to my body. Her legs
cross over mines to lock me in but I'm already a
prisoner to her love. Leaving her doesn't exit my
mouth as we reminisce of our friendships' past. We
rewind moments of us and reveal clues that were
thrown at each other but badly missed. We joke, we
laugh, and we kiss. I pull hair, she grabs me, we kiss
again, but then we slow down and enjoy each other as
friends. We enjoy the friendship that got us here. We
enjoy the friendship it took years to build.

A few moments of silence circulate the atmosphere;
only slight roars of thunder from the rain that has
picked up echoes through the room as we lay.

There's something I need to tell you opens my eyes and interrupt's my daydream of us. Looking down and seeing her beautiful eyes looking back up at me, I could tell that it was serious. You can tell me anything flows from my tongue and relaxes her body as she continues to rub the chest that she lays on; she continues to rub the chest of the man that for years has had a deep desire to be in this position with her. She touches a man that was just in a daydream about her and their future together. She touches a man that was just imagining this moment lasting forever; me and her enjoying each other, facing life together and everything that comes with it. She touches a man that feels blessed to be touched by her, who accepts her for who she is, and who wants to be there with her as she grows further into herself to become who she's supposed to become. She touches me, her friend, and I am ready for whatever she has to tell me.

I LOVE YOU.

Without any explanation, without any previous build up, just I love you. Her voice is soft and even-toned. She was sure of what she was saying. She wasn't just

caught in the moment, she created the moment. From
the phone call, the dinner, to us laying right here right
now was all a plan for her to tell me I love you.
I never would have imagined she felt like that for me.
I never would have thought I would hear I love you
thrust from her heart to my ears with such sincerity
that I became deaf to any other noise around me. All I
could hear was I love you. I love you echoed through
my mind and spirit. I love you bounces around my
memories of us, my desires of us, and the lust I
possessed for her. I love you touches every moment of
our past and made me ask myself did I completely
want what she just gave me? Did I want the
responsibility of her heart?
Did I want her as more than a friend?
Did I want She over You?
I hoped for this moment years ago but not now, not
when I'm in love with You. Not when You are my
everything, my all, my foundation in life. Not when
you are the reason I go home at night regardless. Why
did she tell me this? What did she expect me to say? I
can't say I love you too. We haven't built the

groundwork for that to be real at this time. I didn't even think she looked at me this way. She was just a friend that I secretly had a crush on; I had no idea that she felt this way.

The time allotted for me to reply was occupied by my thoughts so the only response she could receive from her statement was the unmerciful replies of rain and thunder.

She must have felt the wave of my thought patterns for She mentioned You in response to my silence. She mentioned the relationship that I had with You. She understood the value that you possessed in my life. She knew You were the reason why my lips were sealed and why the rain was a symbol of my heart's tears from not being able to say it back. But yet that did not slow She's tongue from forming the underlying value of You compared to her in my life.

She emphasized that she was a better woman in the sense of being a more qualified candidate to represent a letter in the word us. She wanted me. She wanted me for herself. She wanted us to take a stride in becoming more than friends. She assured me that the treatment I received was not temporary, that treating a man like a king was a part of her. She emphasized she needed me to be a part of her and her words made me feel that I wanted to be. Her words convinced me that I wanted to make lying in this bed normality. They convinced me I wanted the excitement that I felt when we talked to be consistent. I've been waiting on the moment when She and I could unify and become us. But was I not being realistic about the situation at hand? Was I allowing myself to be trapped in the moment? Was I giving into exactly what she wanted?

Could I trade my woman?

Could I trade You for Her? Was trading a possibility even with all the history that you and I have?... No. I love you and everything that comes with You. You and I have something that has developed over several years, and I couldn't see myself giving that up because of a moment of lust. Although this was a moment that created a bookmark in She's and I relationship history, it could never outweigh the issues that You and I have been through to help us get to the point where we're at in our relationship.

You had to be ignored so the moment between She and I could happen, but You could never be ignored out of my life. You could never be ignored for her permanently. I just had to get this experience out of my system. I just had to experience She for something that moved inside of me whenever I spoke to her. Something for She inside of me haunted me whenever I was with You. Whenever we talked about the progression of our relationship I thought about She. I always had a question in my mind about She and I had to answer that curiosity. I had to put You to the side for one night for you, me, and her. I had to be selfish so we could progress, so I could progress.

My body language revealed my thoughts as I positioned myself to get up. Sitting on the edge of the bed and thinking about leaving gave me the realization that if I got up and left, things would never be the same; and a part of me needed that. I needed She and I to change so You and I could change. Right then and there I made up my mind.

I came to the conclusion that I was leaving.

Getting up was cut short by a soft hand with a strong grip on my wrist. I turned around slowly because I didn't want to see what I saw. Two beautiful eyes filled with a river of pain flowing down beauty manifested in human form.

Seeing tears in her eyes, hearing "don't leave," crack from her voice was almost too much for me to hold things together. She's my friend and seeing her in pain was painful for me. She didn't physically stop me from removing her arm from her grip but the repeat of "I love you" isolated my bodily functions and molded my feet to the ground so I couldn't do anything else but look at her. Look at her body, feel her pain and wipe her tears from her face. The 'I' in I love you was said with such an emphasis as if she was trying to remind me of our history as well. As if she was reminding me that I've always wanted her. That I've always had a desired for her to be mine in a way that I had You, and that this was my opportunity; the opportunity that my thoughts and actions manifested. This was the opportunity that I've always wanted.....

The opportunity that I thought I've always wanted.

There comes a point in a man's life where a decision
has to be made regardless of how painful it is for all
involved parties. I decided to come here. I decided to
eat, to walk up stairs, and to lay with my friend. I
decided to ignore You for my selfishness. Now I have
to make the decision on which woman I want to
continue my journey throughout life with and I choose
You for the last and final time.

No second thoughts.

Apologies to a broken heart seem pointless at that
moment because we did it to ourselves. We created the
situation every step of the way. We helped each other
feel the best we've ever felt then we turned around and
delivered crushing blows to our dreams, hearts, and
spirits. We stole the happiness from each other like we
never liked each other, like we never cared for each
other, like the love that was hidden never mattered.

In one night dreams were built and shattered.

The right words were hard to locate. The only sound
in the room was coming from the rain illustrating the
tears from broken hearts. The acceptance of her
waving me off is hard. She dismisses my call request

and reveals nothing but her back to me as I continue to get dressed.

One last glance was taken in an attempt for reconciliation; one last look at my friend as I stood at the door silently begging for eye contact. I did love her but not in a way that could be transferred from one relationship to the other. I did want to be with her but at that present time, the time for us had passed. I loved her and I hoped she felt that and I hope her pain heals over time but only time will tell.

Lust, love, and desire were all concealed in her bedroom as I shut the door behind me. With each step down the stairs the heaviness of pain, guilt, and regret got lighter. I was making amends with myself as I got closer to the front door. A change in life can be painful but at the same time necessary. We both needed this night for our individual futures. I commended myself for taking the steps to get She off my mind. I commended myself for being brave enough for my feelings. I commended myself for making the right decision when it was needed the most.

With one last look at the beautiful scene that was put together for me, I silently thanked her for helping me feel better about myself. I thanked her for the memory that we created. I thanked her for her thoughts, for her love.

I thanked her for our moment in time together that will last forever.....

"I walked out of her house and back into the life that I have with you. I apologize if this story hurt you but I felt it was necessary and appropriate for the current situation at hand. We were allowed to express any secrets that would destroy our future marriage if later on discovered, so as a man I felt that you should know the truth about that night when I came home late; about the only time, I ever ignored your phone calls.

I felt you should know the truth about She and I."

The room fell silent as the other two occupants soaked in the vivid recount of a recent past love. My future wife sitting next to me seemed appalled and amazed but still in deep thought. She slowly opens her mouth to speak but Counselor Adams quickly stretches his hand to politely interrupt her. "Um, before you say anything Ms. Jackson there are a few questions that I would like to ask Mr. Evans to obtain a better insight on the situation if you don't mind." She gestures that it's okay to proceed with his job.

Counselor Adams takes his time to speak as he reads over his notes. "Now you two have been together for just about five years and engaged for around seven months am I correct?"

"Yes," I respond quickly as I aim to figure out where he's taking this question and hoping he's going in the direction of where I think he is.

"When did this night with, let's call her by her real name now, Ms. Chanel take place?"

I think about his question and I think about the answer. Then I look at my woman and I think about telling a lie because of the answer. There's only so much truth a person can handle, but a true relationship cannot be built off lies so I proceed with an honest answer.

"About eight months ago." I feel like I am on trial as I complete my statement and slightly glance at my future wife. I can feel her trying to stabilize the uneasiness that has her heart and body shifting right now. She has always been the type to maintain control of her emotions regardless of the situation. That's one of the main reasons why we've been together for so long; we resolve our issues like adults. Hearing my future wife clear her throat to make it clear that she has something to say is heartbreaking because I know what she is about to ask and I have to give her the straight out truth. "So only after a night with her could you propose? She was one of the reasons you were holding back?"

"She was the only reason." I was sincere with my answer but, I wish I could have taken those words back. They came sharp, hard, and fast, but they had to be delivered. I could see her pride trying hard to be the dam that holds back her tears but to no avail. She turned her head to face the window but I could tell that the tears made their way down her face uncontrollably.

I hated seeing my woman cry because she rarely did. I'm starting to feel upset and disappointed at myself for even telling her the story. Maybe it was selfish of me to reveal such a heavy secret but there is something that I need to know; before you ask for something, you have to give a little first. Counselor Adams gave her a minute to get herself together before he continued.

The counselor continues. "Mr. Evans, you do understand that you two have come to premarital counseling to maintain the solid foundation of the relationship that has been built so you will be even more equipped to withstand a long-lasting future together right?" I nod with agreement. "In saying that let me reiterate that my sole purpose for these next few questions is to remove any elephants that may be in the room between the two of you so your marriage can realistically last for the rest of your lives. Now I appreciate your openness and honesty thus far and I'm pretty sure your future wife does as well, but the questions I am about to ask you will dig deep down to unearth the core issues that exist between you, Ms. Chanel, and Ms. Jackson here. Regardless of how difficult it may seem, I need your full cooperation concerning the truth of the matter. Can you two promise me that?" I look at my woman, Erica, that is already on board with an eager expression on her face stating that she wants to know what's in my head and heart. Then I take a look at myself and prepare my mind to reveal all truths that are needed for the progression of our relationship. I'm in love with Erica and only Erica and I believe that with love and God we can last forever. So cockily I raise my chin, "I am ready for all questions that you may have." I look at my future wife, "I'm ready for us to continue to forever." She looks at me seriously with her lips tightly sealed like she has a buildup of questions ready to pour out but her maturity is helping her hold back till it's her turn to speak.

Mr. Adams straightens his glasses and clears his throat before he speaks.

"At the beginning of the story, you stated that some phone calls were ignored with hesitation, was Ms. Jacksons' call included on that list?"

"Yes, they were," I replied.

"I hate to assume so," he looks toward Erica, "Ms. Jackson did you know about Chanel as being a friend of your now-fiancé?"

"Yes, I knew about her and their friendship. I didn't know enough." That word enough was strong and lingering and it came with a look that pierced my heart; that cut my soul but I have to deal with it. I put myself on the hot seat to ease the pressure of future pain. I volunteered the destruction of my trust so the infrastructure of our marriage could be ten times stronger than the relationship that got us to this moment. Her look was hard but I know that there is a sea of words behind her lips that are being held back by a dam of maturity that has me much more nervous about the pain that could potentially arise from her release. There was a reason why I volunteered my story. There was a reason why I openly expressed what could not have otherwise come to light.

There is something in that sea that I need to know.

There is something that I have been fishing for a while now but have yet to discover the answers that she hides from me. I know it may hurt but I need to know. I have to know for my sake, for my sanity, for us.

Counselor Adams continues, "Mr. Evans if you knew that answering Ms. Jackson's' phone call could potentially put you back on the course, obviously you knew where you were headed was wrong, although you state that you and Ms. Chanel are only friends, why continue to head to her house? Why carry out the mission to go see her?"

"Chanel and I were friends before I met Erica but never quite shared the strong emotional attachment that I have developed for my wife, but the friendship that we shared was strong; very strong. We had a type of bond that I've never experienced between a man and a woman before. I'm not sure why and I can't explain it. Yes, we were only friends in the sense that we have never done anything up until that point but it was as if we were soul mates as friends. I could open up to her about things that might change the relationship between me and my wife. I could consult an issue with Chanel and get a woman's point of view before I brought the issue to Erica, so I could have a clear head and not act out of my initial emotions that come with being a man. So when Chanel asked me to come over, the way she said it made it wrong; the way her voice made my insides feel made it wrong. The excitement I felt when she called on that particular day made it wrong. Everything that had something to do with Chanel on that day was wrong in the first place, so a call answered from my woman at that time on that day would have completely changed where I was headed because in my heart I knew how I was feeling about another woman was wrong and I would never want to hurt my woman because of the fairy tale feelings that would have come out of my voice if I would have picked up the phone and told her where I was going. I would have given off that this visit with Chanel was not normal and she would have picked up on my vibe."

"So if it was wrong, why not just go home? What held you back from doing what you felt was right, what you knew was right?" I took a deep breath and gave myself a small pep talk to just continue with the truth, so I can get the truth that I need, "because I was tired of going home in the first place." Counselor Adam's eyes got big for a second but he smoothly transitioned right into the next question like a pro. "Are you tired of the relationship that you have with Ms. Jackson?"

"No."

"Then what are you tired of? Explain what you mean when you refer to the life that you live with Ms. Jackson as normality."

I sit up and adjust myself so I can make sure that I heard correctly because I want to be fully understood because I understand that my answer to this question can alter my relationship out of my control. "I described our relationship as normal because we are in the stage of cruise control in our lives with each other. Yes, we have a great relationship I am perfectly happy but there comes a point after so many years everything is set. We are just us and there is not going to be much change regardless of what surprises that we put on each other. At the end of the day, whether we are home, in California, or London, the final results will be the same; me and her together. Regardless of what kinky surprises we could come up with for each other, they are not needed, so I guess that's why they are not given and I've become accustomed to that; which is why I refer to home as normality. For those reasons, it felt good to receive that from someone I wasn't

expecting. The surprise was that it was from Chanel
not really what she was doing."

"Are you tired of us?" I heard her words but I didn't
look in her direction. I kept my head forward because I
couldn't stand to look into her spirit right now. I can
feel her eyes burning a hole in the side of my mind and
I dare not let my eyes interject with those streams of
emotions. I take a moment and think to myself before I
answer. "No I am not tired of us," I turned and looked
her dead in the eyes, "I love the fact that I can count on
us being together. I love our stability; our guaranteed
companionship. I wouldn't give that up for the world."

Counselor Adams interjects, "Is that the reason you
choose Ms. Jackson over Ms. Chanel? You've known
Ms. Chanel longer than Ms. Jackson why aren't you
two together?"

For a long time, I used to ask myself the same
question. I was infatuated with Chanel since the first
time I saw her walk through the doors of our college
class. She was young, full of energy, and optimistic,
but she knew she was gorgeous. She knew that she
could get what she wanted from any man at any time.

She didn't always take advantage of that but she knew how to use it, and she was a woman with a goal of success in mind and that made her dangerous. So instead of being one of the regular guys that she met and got used and crushed, I just decided to be the real friend that I knew she didn't have. We would have long talks about how guys would approach her and do things for her and sometimes even the heartbreaks that she would endure. In return, I would talk about what was going on in my life. She let me in on the life of a beautiful free-flowing woman, I was curious to know how she lived and I guess she became curious about the stable life I lived. So we kept in touch over the years. For a while, I waited but I felt my position in line was falling further and further away from being not only her number 1 but her only 1. And somewhere along those lines, I met Erica who was just as beautiful but opposite. Erica was a stable wholesome woman. A woman like Erica was raised from the ground up how to treat a man, how to be a great woman on her own but still, have strong family core values installed in her that are openly released for the man that she loves. I knew that being Erica's man came with a piece of mind, stability, and advancement. Secretly I waited for Chanel but then I fell so deep in love with Erica that there was no way I could turn back around. "Chanel and I are not together because of our lives and what we wanted didn't match up. I know what a great woman is and I refuse to be a fool again."

"You proposed to Ms. Jackson roughly a month after your encounter with Ms. Chanel." My heart skipped a beat and my neck stiffened so I couldn't see Erica's reaction to his statement, but he made that sound a lot worse than what it was. But at the same time, I needed him to make that point so I can get closer to the real reason I exploited my most inner secret. I nod agreeably as he continues. "Why did that night with Ms. Chanel make you feel that it was finally the right time to take your relationship to the next level of marriage?" Here we go, now I'm ready to play ball with my future wife. She has been silent but now I need her to talk. "I couldn't bring the thought of another woman into a marriage. At the same time, Erica never pressured me about marriage.

Even after five years she never even mentioned marriage to me and I always thought that was kind of strange. That night with Chanel and I was not completely random, I had thoughts building up for a while, and she just happened to call right on time as my thoughts were wandering back and forth about what to do in my relationship. I've never cheated on my woman until that night but I haven't always felt that monogamy was completely respected in my household." I ended my statement by staring into her eyes and she looked back into mines. My eyes were telling her that I am ready to know. I am ready to hear what's been holding her back from me all these years. Her eyes were screaming back anger; that I would blame my night on her, but she knew what I was talking about. She caught the hint that I threw out and now she felt like she was in a position where she had to talk. I put her back against the wall with my honesty now it was her turn.....

. . . .

Looking at my future husband stare at me with such fire and intent in his eyes almost made me weak in the knees. I knew what he wanted to know. I finally realized why we were here. Why he delivered a heartbreaking story that crushed my world in one solid blow. I always felt that he and Chanel had something for each other, but I was confident in our love, I was confident that our love would bring him home every night, and it did. Even if he brought her home with him, he came home, and that's what I needed, that's what made me happy; a man who came home.

Now Counselor Adams addressed his attention to me. Now it was my turn for the questions. "Ms. Jackson, I am not here to compare what is normal and what is not, so I'll be frank and ask, is marriage important to you? Please be honest."

Daniel's eyes have yet to lose their grip on mine. He had a look on his face that he was not going to miss a single word or expression that came from me. He set this entire thing up for this moment of honesty from me. I hate that we had to get to this point but some things should just be left in the dark. Some things a woman just has to figure out on her own. But if honesty is what he needs then I guess I will just have to give it to him the way he wants it. He has been pressuring me about the topic for a while now. I guess he knows me in the sense that I was protecting his feelings which is why I guess he didn't spare mines when I wish he had of. "Yes, marriage is very important to me. I came from a two parent home. I understand the values and importance of marriage. I knew Daniel was going to be my husband shortly after we got together. I recognized the way he loved me and I knew what kind of man he was. I knew that he was the one for me."

"Then why not even mention marriage to a man that loves you after five long years?"

I knew that question was coming and I could do nothing but break eye contact from Daniel who was now biting his thumbnail from nervousness because of my answer to come. I looked off and tears began to form in my eyes. I could feel the pressure of the pain to come. I know the truth is going to hurt me and

Daniel, but I have to say it. Shaking my head, "because of him." The realization of that answer hit me and hit me hard. I just realized that I have been holding back my life with Daniel because of another man.

"Explain to me what happened that night." Daniel pleaded. "Explain to me what happened that night that you left me, please."

"Daniel it's not what you think it is."

"I need to know." His plead cracked from emotions. The hurt of not knowing was spilling out into his words. I could feel his tears flowing down his face. He needed me to tell him the truth. I have no choice but to tell him the truth.

"I can remember that night like it was last night.....

ABOUT THE AUTHOR

I grew up in Atlanta GA. Inspired by the poetic notions that travel through my mind whenever I see love, I began to write poetry. From there my poetic aspirations lead me to engage in book writing. This is my first book and the first part of things to come. I would like to thank everybody who read the book and I will enjoy engaging with you to answer any questions or respond to your feedback. Email me at Danielwriteseverything@gmail.com.
Thank you.

Made in the USA
Middletown, DE
13 August 2024

58619754R00028